Ella and One Tiny Thing

To Sandy,
Thank you for your
service to the community.
I look forward to working
more with you!
Best,
C.L. FAILS

written and illustrated
by C. L. Fails

To ALL who have ever wondered about the significance of their presence, words, and actions - this book is for you.

"The world is so BIG and I am so small," whispered young Ella, who stood just three feet tall.

"What's that my dear?" asked her mom with great cheer.

"Why does it matter what I choose to do?"
asked Ella.

"But HOW mom?" asked Ella.

She listened as her mom dropped one pebble into the still water and said...

"Just one thing, one tiny thing has a ripple effect on us all.
Some of the biggest things in the world
start from something so tiny and small."

Ella watched the ripples dance gracefully across the water.

"Go ahead," said mom, "name something itsy bitsy."

Ella put on her thinking cap.

"A TWIG!" she shouts,
"A twig isn't big!"
"You're right," says her mom with a smile.

"Though one twig from a tree
gives a home to a bird.
It's a nest when they're put in a pile."

"Just one thing, one tiny thing has a ripple effect on us all.
Some of the biggest things in the world
start from something so tiny and small."

"A seed," shouts Ella, "a seed isn't big!"
"You're right," says her mom once again.

"Though a seed gives us plants
that can turn into food,
to feed us and all of our friends," said mom.

"What else comes from a seed?"
she asked little Ella.
"Well a seed can become a gigantic tree
that will grow BIG and TALL in the sun."

"Then that tree," says her mom,
"will provide us with shade
so we'll linger outside 'til there's none."

"Just one thing, one tiny thing has a ripple effect on us all.
Some of the biggest things in the world
start from something so tiny and small."

"Well it starts in my head then it GROWS!"
Ella shouted with excitement.

"It grows when I dream and
it grows when I squint and
it grows when I scratch my chin.
The more that I think,
the bigger it gets."

"Then that's when you dig down and begin," finished mom.

"SEE IT!"
"DREAM IT!"
DO IT!"

"Yes, it all begins with you!"
said mom.

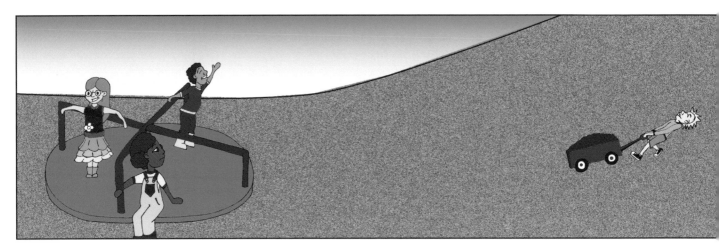

Be the tree and shelter someone. Be the twig in someone's home.

Be the pebble, start the journey of the waves that spread and roam.

You my dear, can be that beacon
that bright light that shines above.
Just one thing, one tiny thing
can lift the world to hope and love.

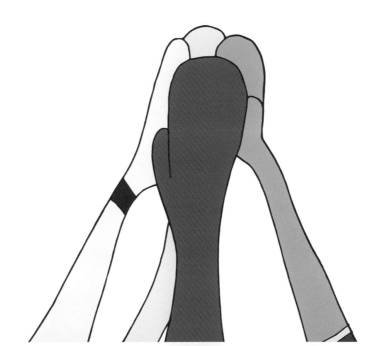

"And that's why it matters what you do,"
said mom,
as Ella gave her the biggest hug she knew.

CPSIA information can be obtained at www.ICGtesting.com
Printed in the USA
LVIW01n1106130215
426935LV00010B/18

* 9 7 8 0 9 8 8 6 6 8 9 2 8 *